Princesses and Peas

A Christmas Love Story

Terry Boucher

ISBN: Softcover   978-1-7960-3406-6
        Hardcover   978-1-7960-3831-6
        EBook   978-1-7960-3405-9

This is a work of fiction. Names, characters,
places and incidents either are the product of the
author's imagination or are used fictitiously, and any
resemblance to any actual persons, living or dead,
events, or locales is entirely coincidental.

Print information available on the last page

Rev. date: 05/15/2019

To order additional copies of this book, contact:
Xlibris
1-888-795-4274
www.Xlibris.com
Orders@Xlibris.com

For Julie, Jessica, and Elizabeth

Chapter 1

Planning a Party

Once upon a time, but not too, too long ago, there lived a fine young gentleman named Kevin. Kevin's father, Matthew, was the king of Athanasia, a small kingdom in the Northern Lands. Being the son of the king made Kevin a prince in this land, and he was held in high esteem in the country where they lived.

The Christmas season was upon them, and Prince Kevin's mother, Queen Victoria, was busy planning for their big Christmas dinner. They had a great tradition of inviting friends over for dinner on Christmas Day. Then after dinner, everyone gathered in the parlor for songs while enjoying a warm fire. The guests would stay late into the evening and then spend the night. King Matthew's palace was big and had many guest rooms. It was always a joyous occasion. King Matthew felt it was important to mark the birthday of Jesus in such a festive way. And since he was the king, it was considered a great honor to be invited to this party.

One day in early December, Queen Victoria was speaking with Kevin about the Christmas party. She said, "Kevin, maybe we should invite a young maiden of good family to our Christmas party this year. Perhaps she will turn out to be a true princess, and you can marry her. Only a true princess is good enough for my son. And with you just turning twenty-two, it is time you started thinking about these things."

"Oh, Mother, please don't try to push me into marriage," replied Kevin. "Besides, how would you know if the girl were a true princess?"

Queen Victoria said, "A true princess is so delicate that she could feel a pea in her bed even underneath three mattresses, and then she would not be able to sleep."

"Very well," said Kevin. "Invite whomever you please. I am always happy to meet new people anyway. But the decision to marry must be left to me and to the young lady."

"Of course, my dear. I only want for you to be happy," replied Queen Victoria.

Queen Victoria liked being the wife of the king. She cherished all the ceremony that came with the position. And so she was determined to make sure Prince Kevin married a young lady from a proper family. King Matthew, on the other hand, was more practical. He enjoyed being the king because it gave him a chance to serve the people. And he had little patience for people who only cared about him because of the prestige knowing the king gave them.

Unknown to either Queen Victoria or Prince Kevin, Mr. Cane, a new provincial mayor in King Matthew's region of the country, was waiting in the room next door. Mr. Cane was basically a good man, but he liked the prestige that came with being a mayor. And he was always looking for ways to move even higher into society. He had come to meet with King Matthew and had overheard Queen Victoria telling Kevin about the way to determine a true princess with a pea.

Mr. Cane then went in to meet with King Matthew, who invited Queen Victoria to come in and meet the new mayor.

"I am delighted to meet you, my lady," said Mr. Cane. "My wife, Jane, and my daughter, Dorothy, find this region of the country simply charming."

"Oh, you have a daughter. How lovely! And how old is Dorothy?" asked Queen Victoria.

"Why, she has just turned twenty. A beautiful young lady she is, if I do say so myself," answered Mr. Cane.

Queen Victoria's eyes grew bright. A twenty-year-old young woman of good family would be just the person for Kevin to meet. "Well, Mr. Cane, you and your family will have to join us for Christmas dinner and then enjoy songs with us afterward. We have plenty of guest rooms to accommodate your family."

Mr. Cane was overjoyed at the invitation and gladly accepted. He saw this as an opportunity to introduce Dorothy to Kevin. A marriage between his daughter and the king's son would guarantee his position in the upper circles of society.

When he got home, Mr. Cane told his wife and daughter about the invitation to Christmas dinner. He was sure to tell Dorothy, "Check under your bed before you go to sleep. Queen Victoria plans to hide a pea under the mattresses. She thinks that a true princess can feel a pea under three mattresses. I think this is nonsense, but let's play along. It could be to our advantage. If you find a pea under the bottom mattress, you must act as if you did not sleep a wink in the morning."

Dorothy liked the finer things in life, and she thought that by marrying the king's son, she would always have nice things. So she agreed to the plan.

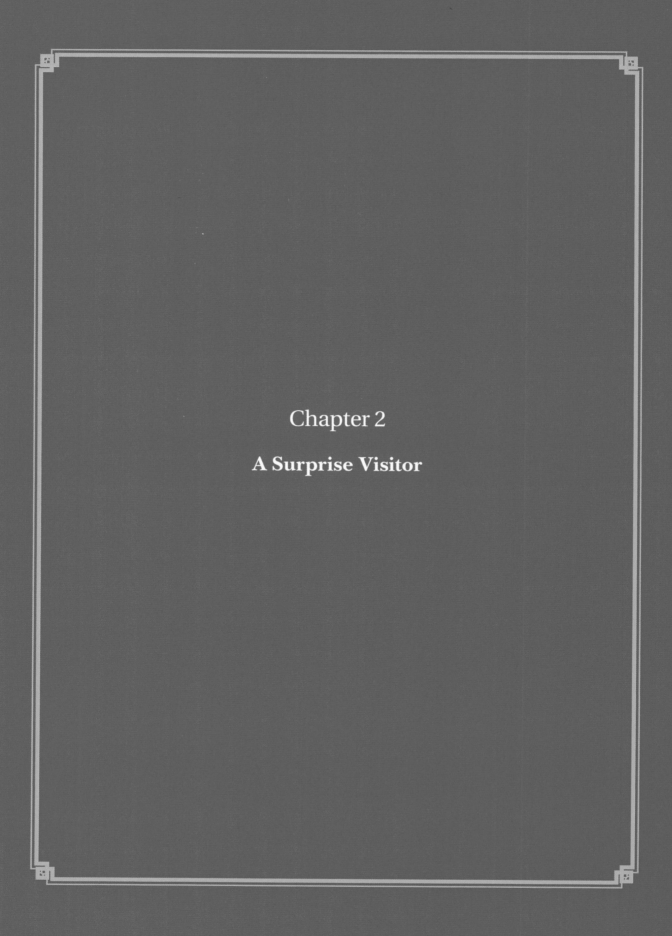

Chapter 2

A Surprise Visitor

On Christmas Eve, Queen Victoria and Kevin, along with their staff, were busily putting the finishing touches on their decorations. An unexpected snowstorm had come upon the village and brought with it about a foot of freshly fallen snow.

"Oh, we are going to have a delightful white Christmas. It will be so beautiful," exclaimed Queen Victoria.

"Yes, it will be great!" agreed Kevin.

It was getting close to afternoon teatime. Queen Victoria asked one of the butlers to go out to the well to get water for tea.

But Kevin interrupted and said to the butler, "It's Christmas Eve, and it's cold outside. Please, stay inside where it's warm and let me go instead." So Kevin fetched his coat and a bucket and headed out to the well.

While he was drawing the water, a lovely young woman with beautiful blonde hair and blue eyes came up to him. She was wearing traveling clothes. "Excuse me, kind sir, but my carriage seems to be stuck in a high snowbank on the road. My brother is trying to get it out, but the snow is just too deep! Can someone please help us?" pleaded the young lady. "I don't want to disturb the king or his family, as I am sure they are busy preparing for Christmas. But perhaps you can help us!"

Kevin looked at the young woman and was mesmerized for a moment. She was so beautiful that he struggled to come to his senses. But he regained his composure and said, "It is late in the day, and it will be dark very soon. It would be hard to try to dig you out now. Please get your brother and invite him in; you can spend the night with us. The roads are slippery after this storm, and surely you will get stuck again. Christmas Eve is no time to be traveling in the dark. We will dig you out first thing in the morning and have you on your way."

"Thank you, kind sir, but I don't want to impose on the king's holiday celebration. I'm no one important. I'd feel out of place," said the young lady. "Perhaps we can eat in the kitchen and not be a bother to anyone."

"Don't be silly," said Kevin. "Christmas is a time for caring and sharing. What better way to do this than to help a stranger in need? And, yes, King Matthew would welcome you with open arms. Please, let me introduce myself. I am Prince Kevin, and King Matthew is my father. What is your name, Miss?"

The young lady's face blushed. She never dreamed that the prince himself would be drawing water from the well. She gently bowed and said, "Your Highness, my name is Taryn. My brother's name is James. Thank you so much for your hospitality; I am humbled by your kindness." Taryn had just turned twenty years old, and James was seventeen.

Taryn and Kevin went to the carriage to get James and the horse. They brought the horse to the stable and headed for the house. Once Taryn and James had come inside and warmed themselves, Queen Victoria invited them to supper. She instructed Taryn to go with the maid and get a nice dress to wear so that she wouldn't have to remain in her traveling clothes.

While at supper, King Matthew asked why the brother and sister were traveling all alone in such weather.

"I have a childhood friend who now lives in this village. She wrote to me and told me she had broken her leg, and I wanted to visit her to cheer her for Christmas. James accompanied me on the trip, and our plan was to return home this afternoon so that we would be there for Christmas Eve. We did not know this storm was coming."

"Well, what a lovely act of Christmas charity for your friend," said King Matthew. "'Tis a fine thing to do, lass. Isn't it, Kevin?"

"Why yes, Father, it is," replied the boy. He suspected his father was up to something.

King Matthew thought Taryn was a lovely girl and wanted to point out her kindness to Kevin. Queen Victoria was happy to be hospitable to Taryn, but she had her mind set on matching Kevin with Dorothy, who would be coming the next day. Although this Taryn seemed nice enough, Queen Victoria did not think she was a member of high society, partly because she had arrived wearing plain traveling clothes and was traveling without a valet. Still, she wanted to be sure, so she instructed the maid to give Taryn the same room that they had prepared for Dorothy for the next night and to be sure to put a pea underneath the bottom mattress.

After supper, King Matthew invited Taryn and James to join the family in the sitting room. He asked Taryn what she liked to do.

"I love to read," she said.

"Wonderful!" exclaimed King Matthew. "About what?"

"Oh, all kinds of things," answered Taryn. "I really like to read about history, to learn about how people lived long ago. I also like to read fantasy adventure stories, where people are faced with challenges, and then they find the strength to overcome them. There are wonderful stories about mermaids and fairies and wizards who fight for good against bad."

Kevin's eyes opened wide in surprise. He jumped into the conversation, saying, "Why, I love to read too. I also like history and adventure stories. I just finished reading a story about people who live on other planets and travel through space to see different worlds."

"Life on other planets! Oh, how fascinating. I love stories that create completely new places, but that one creates completely new worlds!" exclaimed Taryn with a look of genuine excitement. "My dream is to teach children to read so that I can open their eyes to all these new worlds hidden in books. Maybe someday I can even write my own book," she proclaimed.

Kevin replied, "That is a wonderful dream. Hopefully it will come true for you." Kevin was really beginning to like this beautiful girl who'd just mysteriously shown up at his house this afternoon.

A little later, Kevin showed Taryn the library that was in the king's palace.

"Oh, this is so wonderful!" She exclaimed. "So many books, and all right under your own roof! I could live in this room and never leave."

Kevin said, "Yes, there are advantages to being the king's son." He was very happy at Taryn's reaction to the library.

Kevin and Taryn spent a long time talking and laughing about different stories that they had read and adventures they would like to have on their own. Kevin felt very much alive talking with Taryn.

Eventually, Queen Victoria broke into their conversation and said, "Kevin, it is time for our annual Christmas Eve tradition where your father reads the Christmas story by the fireplace. Please join us, Taryn. Your brother James has already taken a seat near the fire."

King Matthew began reading the story.

"The angel Gabriel appeared to a young girl named Mary, who lived in a town called Nazareth. He greeted her, 'Hail, Mary, full of grace, the Lord is with you.' But Mary was very afraid. The angel said to her, 'Fear not Mary, for I bring you joyful news. God is very happy with you, and would like you to become the mother of his Son. His name will be Jesus, and He will be a Savior to all people.' Mary replied, 'I am the maidservant of the Lord. May it be done to me as you say.' With that the angel left her.

"Mary was betrothed to Joseph, a carpenter. Soon after they were married, and then they learned that Caesar Augustus had passed a law saying that everyone must go to their hometown to be counted in a census so that they could pay taxes to Rome.

"Joseph's hometown was Bethlehem, so they had to travel from Nazareth to Bethlehem. Mary rode on a donkey. When they got to Bethlehem, there was no room in the inn, so they had to spend the night in a stable with the animals. Mary gave birth to Jesus that night. Because they had no crib, she laid him in a manger, with hay for his mattress.

"That same night, an angel appeared to shepherds who were watching their flocks on the hillside. The angel told the shepherds to go to Bethlehem to see the newborn king lying in a manger. They hurried to Bethlehem and found Joseph and Mary in the stable, and they fell in adoration of Jesus lying in the manger. They told Joseph and Mary about the angel's message. And Mary remembered this and treasured it in her heart.

"A little later, three wise men came from the east to see Jesus. They were following a new, bright star that led them to Bethlehem. They offered Jesus gifts of gold, myrrh, and frankincense. These were gifts fit for a king, a newborn king. Then the wise men returned to their country, praising God."

"Of all the stories I have ever read or heard," said Kevin, "this one is the best."

"And it is true," added King Matthew.

Taryn said, "And I must thank you, King Matthew and Queen Victoria, for giving us shelter on this Christmas Eve so that James and I did not have to sleep in a stable. I can appreciate how Mary and Joseph felt that night as they were looking for shelter."

"You are very welcome, child," said King Matthew.

"Oh my, it is getting late," exclaimed Queen Victoria. "We had all better get to bed."

The butler came to show James to his room. The maid came to show Taryn to her room, but Queen Victoria interrupted, saying, "Thank you, but I will show Taryn to her room myself. That will give me a chance to chat with our young visitor a little."

"Of course, my lady," said the maid.

Taryn was surprised to hear this, and a little nervous. The queen herself wanted to chat with her. She wondered in amazement what further surprises this Christmas Eve would hold for her.

Queen Victoria really wanted to be sure that Taryn made it to the proper guest room with the pea under the mattress. She was going to see to this personally. So Queen Victoria walked with Taryn to the room with the pea under the three mattresses. They chatted while walking. Queen Victoria found Taryn to be quite charming for a common village girl.

When the reached the proper guest room, Queen Victoria said, "Sleep well, my child. Merry Christmas."

"Thank you, my lady. Merry Christmas to you too," answered Taryn.

Chapter 3

A Restless Night

Taryn went to bed, and although she was tired, she had trouble sleeping. She tossed and turned for much of the night, and she could not figure out why. Part of the time she was thinking about her parents and how worried they must be about her and James. She also spent time thinking about the evening and her conversation with Kevin. It was wonderful to talk with someone who shared so many of her interests. He had been so nice and kind to her. But he was the king's son, and Taryn was sure he had plenty of girls from high society pursuing him. He would never be interested in a simple girl like her. And yet, didn't Christmas miracles happen? She allowed herself to keep just a little bit of hope alive in her heart.

Eventually she did fall asleep, but morning came very soon. Although Taryn felt very tired from her poor night's sleep, she did not want to offend her hosts; she made sure to wash her face and comb her hair well so that she could appear as wide awake as possible. However, because she was tired, she forgot to put on her lovely heart necklace. She left it on the dresser in the guest room.

When she came down to breakfast, Kevin, James, and Queen Victoria were already at the table.

"Good morning, Taryn. Merry Christmas!" greeted Kevin. They all exchanged Christmas greetings.

As Taryn sat down, Queen Victoria asked how her sleep was. She was anxious to see if the pea had disturbed her during the night. Even Kevin's ears perked at the question.

But Taryn, not wanting to seem like an ungracious guest, simply said, "Why, I had a very pleasant night's sleep. I dreamed of Christmas fairies dancing under the moonlight and greeting elves who were bringing presents."

Kevin's heart dropped at the answer. To tell the truth, so did Queen Victoria's heart. Even though she thought Taryn was just a commoner, she did think she was a lovely girl and would have been pleasantly surprised to find that she really was a true princess.

Queen Victoria simply responded to Taryn, "Why what a lovely dream to have on the night before Christmas."

King Matthew came into the room. After offering Christmas greetings, he said, "I will have the staff dig out your carriage. After Christmas Mass, Kevin will take you to your carriage. The roads are clear today, and I am sure your parents are terribly worried."

"Yes, I'm sure they are," Taryn agreed.

After breakfast, they all went to church for Christmas mass. King Matthew and Queen Victoria went in one coach, and Kevin took Taryn and James in another coach. The staff went to dig out the carriage, so Kevin hitched Taryn and James's horse to the back of his coach so that he could be hitched to their carriage afterward.

Kevin liked Christmas Mass because it was one of the most beautiful celebrations of the whole year. The church was decorated with poinsettias, and the manger scene was on display. The songs were the happy Christmas songs. They always opened with "O Come, All Ye Faithful" and closed with "Joy to the World."

After Mass, Kevin took Taryn and James to their carriage. On the way, Kevin asked Taryn about her family. Taryn said that her father was a carpenter and that he had helped build many of the houses in their village. Her mother was a librarian; that was why Taryn spent so much time in the library and developed her love of stories.

They hitched their horse to the carriage and pulled it out of the snowbank. While James was loading their bags into the carriage, Kevin pulled out a small present and gave it to Taryn. "Since it is Christmas morning, and you have had quite a night missing your family, I was hoping this would make you feel a little better."

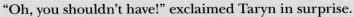

"Oh, you shouldn't have!" exclaimed Taryn in surprise.

"It really is just a small token," said Kevin.

Taryn opened the package. There was a book inside. It was about a knight who traveled to a faraway land to help the local king defeat a gang of bandits. While there, he fell in love with a young woman who lived there but was considered to be too much of a commoner to marry a knight. The story was about his struggle to help the king while also trying to win the heart of this woman, despite the disapproval of the people in the kingdom about their relationship.

"This is one of my favorite stories, and I wanted to share it with you since we both seem to love adventure stories."

"I am sure I will love it," said Taryn. "You have been so very kind to us, and we were just strangers. You are truly a royal prince, Your Highness!"

"It was nothing. I am sure you would have done the same. And please, just call me Kevin. 'Your Highness' is much too formal for a young man like me," replied Kevin.

"Oh, I wouldn't feel comfortable doing that. How about Prince Kevin?" pleaded Taryn.

"Deal!" said Kevin.

James came and told Taryn that they should be going. "We don't have that long of a journey to get home. We should be there by early afternoon."

Kevin took Taryn's hand and helped her into the carriage. Taryn looked into his deep blue eyes as he held her hand. He looked back into her crystal clear blue eyes as well and gave her a smile. She blushed and turned away.

"Where do your parents live?" asked Kevin.

"In the next village over, near the center of town. That makes it easy for my mother to get to the library," replied Taryn.

"Well, take care," said Kevin. "Merry Christmas."

"Farewell. Thank you again so very much for your hospitality. Merry Christmas to you too!" said Taryn as they drove away.

Kevin watched them go, and then turned toward home. He became aware of many different feelings flowing through him. He felt very glad and very sad at the same time, and he didn't quite know why. He couldn't stop thinking about Taryn and what a nice time he had talking to her and sharing his stories with her. He wished she didn't have to go, and yet he knew she did. She belonged with her family on Christmas, not with a group of strangers.

Chapter 4

A Christmas Party

When Kevin got home, his mother told him to come into the parlor, for it was time to open their presents. The joy of opening gifts with the family took Kevin's mind off of missing Taryn for a while. And Kevin got a new adventure book as a gift—a book about pirates and a brave captain in the king's Navy who tried to stop them.

It was now midafternoon, and guests would be arriving anytime. As they arrived, the guests came into the parlor. Mr. and Mrs. Cane and Dorothy arrived and were escorted into the party. The guests were enjoying some snacks before dinner. Queen Victoria brought Kevin to meet Dorothy.

"Oh, Kevin, this is Dorothy. She is the daughter of Mayor Cane. Their family is new to the area, so would you please show Dorothy around the house and make her feel at home?"

"Why, yes, of course," said Kevin. "I am very pleased to meet you," he said to Dorothy.

"The pleasure is mine, Your Highness," responded Dorothy.

Since Kevin was a friendly person and a fine young gentleman, he would have been happy to show anyone around. But given that Dorothy was a very pretty young woman with beautiful long red hair and bright green eyes, this would indeed be a pleasure for him. He did think about Taryn, but he tried to tell himself that meeting Taryn had been just a chance event, and he may never see her again. And here was a young woman who, in addition to being very pretty, was also a mayor's daughter, which meant she was of a good family. This should make his mother happy. Kevin was not aware that his mother was actually trying to match him with Dorothy.

Kevin showed Dorothy around the house. Dorothy was very impressed with the Christmas decorations. In every room they went into, she commented on how lovely they were. When they got to the library, Kevin showed her the bookcases where he kept all of his favorite stories. Dorothy listened attentively, but since she was not as avid a reader as Kevin, she had little to contribute to this part of the conversation. She certainly didn't react the way Taryn had reacted to the library. As she was looking around the room, she noticed a book about ballet on one of the shelves. She took the book off the shelf and started looking at it, forgetting that Kevin was even there.

Just then, the butler came and called them to dinner. Kevin escorted Dorothy to the dining room. The table was beautifully set with fine dishes, glasses, and silverware. Each guest had three forks, two knives, and a spoon. There was a knife and fork for salad, a knife and fork for dinner, a fork for dessert, and a spoon for tea. Dorothy remarked about how wonderful everything looked.

Dorothy loved decorating and dancing. She had taken ballroom dance lessons as a child, as did all the children of high society; but Dorothy had also taken some ballet lessons. She would be very happy to marry someone who had a fine house she could decorate and also who could take her to see ballets and allow her to continue taking dancing lessons herself. Kevin could certainly give her a fine house, but was he interested in ballet like she was? She did not know.

Once everyone was seated, King Matthew said grace. "Bless us, oh, Lord, on this Christmas Day, and these thy gifts, which we are about to receive from thy bounty. Through Christ our Lord, Amen."

They started with salad, rolls, and shrimp cocktails. For the main course, they had turkey with gravy, mashed potatoes, corn, stuffing, and green beans with almonds in them. For dessert, they had apple and pumpkin pie with whipped cream. All the food was very delicious.

Dorothy was seated right next to Kevin. During dinner, Queen Victoria asked her how she had liked the tour of the house. Dorothy told her how she'd loved all of the decorations and how her mother had taught her all about proper interior decorating. Then Dorothy asked Queen Victoria if the ballet book she had found in the library was hers. Queen Victoria said that she had gotten that book when she was a little girl and her mother had taken her to see the ballet. Dorothy and Queen Victoria had a lovely conversation, but other than a few polite exchanges, Dorothy and Kevin hardly talked at all.

Kevin was thinking about Taryn and how easy it was to talk to her. He was thinking about some of the stories they'd both had read and how they'd shared their feelings about them. Suddenly King Matthew said, "I guess it must be time to go into the parlor. Kevin is just sitting there staring into space."

Kevin blushed because he was thinking about Taryn. But the other people assumed he must have blushed because he was sitting next to Dorothy. "Why, yes, Father. Let's go now and start the carol singing," he said.

The guests moved into the parlor. King Matthew sat at the piano and starting playing. The first song they sang was "Joy to the World." They also sang "Hark the Herald Angels Sing," "Oh Little Town of Bethlehem," and "Away in a Manger." The fire was warm, and the Christmas tree was sparkling with lots of pretty ornaments.

After many songs, stories, and Christmas cookies, it was time to go to bed.

Kevin wished Dorothy a good night. Queen Victoria showed her to her room, just as she had done the night before with Taryn. "We have an extra special room for so lovely a young lady," she said to Dorothy as she showed her into the room with the bed that had the pea under the three mattresses. "Pleasant dreams," she said as she left Dorothy alone and headed for her own room.

Once Dorothy was alone, she changed into her nightgown and got ready for bed. Before getting into bed, she checked under the mattresses and saw the pea, just as her father had suspected.

She climbed into bed and said her prayers and then lay down. She thought about what a lovely house this was and how nice Queen Victoria was. If only she could get Kevin to marry her, then she would be able to live in this beautiful house. Soon she was fast asleep.

Before returning to her own bedroom, Queen Victoria stopped by Kevin's room. Kevin was still up. She said, "Isn't Dorothy a very pretty girl? I think she would be very good for you, dear."

"Yes, she is pretty, but I don't know. We didn't seem to have that much in common," Kevin replied.

"Nonsense," cried Queen Victoria. "You can tell she has had a good upbringing just like you. You just need a little time to get to know her. We will see in the morning if she is a true princess or not. Good night."

"Good night, Mother," said Kevin, and he got ready for bed and went to sleep.

Chapter 5

A True Princess?

The next day, Kevin awoke, got dressed, and went down to the kitchen for breakfast. The cook was preparing scrambled eggs served with toast and fresh strawberries. Kevin sat down and started eating. His mother came into the room and sat next to him. She greeted him by saying, "Good morning, dear!"

But poor Kevin almost hadn't even noticed that his mother had come into the room. Looking half-startled, he quickly replied, "Oh! Why hello, Mother. Yes, good morning to you too." Kevin had a lot on his mind. Just two days earlier, he hadn't had a care in the world. He was free and easy, and Christmas was coming. But now, a mere two days later, he had two women on his mind. First came Taryn, a beautiful girl who had mysteriously appeared at their home and who seemed to have a great deal in common with him. But she obviously was not a princess, and his mother seemed intent on his marrying a princess.

Next came Dorothy, who was also a beautiful woman and who clearly fit very well into the world in which Kevin and his family lived. And Dorothy seemed to be a nice person. Yet it seemed that he had to work harder at talking with her.

***

Dorothy woke up and noticed the sun shining brightly in the window. She'd had a very restful sleep. As she was stretching the last bit of sleep out, she remembered the pea. She thought to herself that she must appear downstairs looking as if she hadn't slept well. She then stopped for a minute and said to herself, "Dorothy, what are you doing? This seems like the wrong way to get a man to marry you!" But she didn't want to disappoint her father, and she very much wanted to live in this nice house, so she put her second thoughts aside.

Quickly she got up and threw on her bathrobe. She looked in the mirror and made her hair look messy. Then she took some brown eye shadow and put it under her eyes to make it look like she had dark circles from lack of sleep. She then headed downstairs to breakfast.

She came into the kitchen looking a bit flustered. Queen Victoria spoke to her first. "Well good morning, child! How did you sleep last night?"

"Oh, I guess I'm just too used to my own bed at home. I just could not get comfortable last night," replied Dorothy. "But I don't want to sound like an ungrateful guest."

"Oh, what a shame. Well, just sit here next to Kevin, and breakfast will be served. And don't worry about sounding ungrateful. You are our guest, and we want you to be comfortable." Although she tried to sound concerned, Queen Victoria smiled inside.

Of course, Kevin's ears perked at Dorothy's words as well. He knew all about the pea. Suddenly he wondered if maybe Dorothy was a true princess and if maybe he should work harder on getting to know her better. Still, he was a little saddened at the thought that he would probably never see Taryn again. But he would really have no reason to see her, and if Dorothy were a true princess, why would he need to?

He started thinking that perhaps he had read too many fantasy stories and that any dreams he had of Taryn were silly. It was time for him to grow up and start living in the real world. Dorothy was here now, she was beautiful, and she appeared to be a true princess. And this would please his mother.

Kevin and Dorothy talked pleasantly during breakfast. Then she got dressed and prepared to leave for home with her parents.

Queen Victoria told King Matthew to invite the Cane family over for New Year's Eve, when they were planning to have dinner and dancing to bring in the New Year. Mr. and Mrs. Cane graciously accepted. So as the Canes were leaving, Kevin told Dorothy he would look forward to seeing her later that week at the New Year's Eve party. Dorothy said she was looking forward to it.

Kevin felt he had made the right decision to forget about Taryn and focus his thoughts on Dorothy. This just seemed to be better for everyone involved.

***

When their carriage had gotten away from the king's palace, Mr. Cane turned to Dorothy and said, "Things are going just wonderfully! You did a great job making them think you couldn't sleep. Queen Victoria surely must think you are a true princess."

"Yes, Father. I did just as you asked me to do." Although things seemed to be working out as they had hoped, Dorothy still felt a little uncomfortable. She did not like deceiving people. In her heart, Dorothy really was a nice and honest person. "Father, do you really think this is the best way for me to get Kevin to like me, by lying to him?" she asked.

Mr. Cane replied, "Dorothy, this is very important to me. Besides, this is just a little white lie. No one is going to get hurt by it. And look what we stand to gain."

Dorothy didn't want to disappoint her father, and she did love Kevin's house. Maybe this would be her chance. It seemed to be the only way to get into the upper circle of society, so she convinced herself that there was nothing wrong with what they were doing.

Chapter 6

Christmas Dreams

It was now afternoon on the day after Christmas. Over in the next village, Taryn went into town to visit with her mother at the town library. "To what do I owe this nice visit, my dear?" said her mother.

"Oh, I just had to get out of the house, Mother," explained Taryn. "I didn't know what to do with myself."

"You have been like this ever since you came home yesterday," said her mother. "Your father and I were worried sick about the two of you when you didn't make it home on Christmas Eve. But not only was there nothing to worry about, you in fact had a grand time being entertained at the king's palace by the prince. Ever since then your head has been in the clouds."

"He was just so wonderful and so nice to me. And we had such a lovely conversation about books and life. Oh, I can't get him out of my mind. But I must. I'm just a simple girl from a small village, and he is the prince. I am sure I will never see him again. He's probably forgotten about me already."

"Oh, my dear, sweet child. Don't sell yourself short. You're a fine, beautiful young lady. You'll be a fine catch for any young man, even a prince! I know it seems unlikely that you'll see this handsome Prince Kevin again, and maybe that is what is meant to be. In the meantime, don't worry about the future. Just enjoy this as a special memory and a blessing that you found the help you needed when you were stranded in the cold. Love will come in its own time," said her mother comfortingly. "And who knows? Our Lord works in mysterious ways. If it is to be, he will find a way to get the two of you together."

"Oh, I sure hope so. I'm hoping with all my heart that maybe, somehow, there's a way for me to meet him again." Taryn's eyes were watering, and her heart was pounding at the thought.

Taryn spent the week reading the book that Kevin had given her. She treasured the story. She could relate to the part about a knight trying to marry a common girl. That was what she was hoping right now, that Prince Kevin could be her knight in shining armor. She knew it was unlikely. But somewhere in her heart, every time she held that book, she could feel Kevin's hand holding hers as he had done while helping her into the carriage on Christmas. She was hoping beyond hope, and her hope became a prayer, and the angels heard it.

On the night before New Year's Eve, Taryn was sitting in bed reading the last pages of the book Kevin had given her. The knight and the king had defeated the bandits and recovered the treasure that had been stolen. The king offered the knight a handsome reward to take back with him to his homeland.

But the knight said to the king, "Sire, I have fought alongside you for truth and justice. I have risked my life for your kith and kin. I must now speak the truth to you. No reward of gold can fill me now. The only treasure I want is the heart of this fair maiden. I know she is of common station, but that matters not to me, for she has been kind and caring. In my eyes, her love is worth more than all the gold in the world. My life would be worthless if I could not have her for my bride. Please give me your consent, and I will take her with me, to live as my wife, and all will be even."

The king said, "Who am I to stand in the way of true love? You have been a true friend of this land. I shall not deny your request. Go. Take this maiden's hand and make her your wife. You have my blessing on this. Fare thee well."

Taryn thought to herself, *That is how I hoped the story would end. Oh, if only my story would end that way. I would be so happy.* She blew out the candle, snuggled into her blankets, and drifted off to sleep.

While she was sleeping, she dreamed that Kevin was the knight and she was the common maiden. He was dressed in fine clothes, but she was in common working clothes. He reached for her hand, but the townspeople pulled her away, saying, "Remember your place, common girl."

She turned to flee in shame, but another hand grabbed hers. It was King Matthew, dressed as the king in the story. He said, "Don't run away, sweet child. I grant your wish. You are now a princess."

And with that, her working clothes transformed into a beautiful gown. The king presented her to the knight, who took her hand and led her into a dance. They danced as if they were the only two people in the world. He then took her on his horse, and the two of them rode away into the sunset.

Taryn woke up the next day feeling very refreshed. It was New Year's Eve. One more day until the New Year! Taryn didn't quite understand why, but she suddenly felt that something very special was going to happen in the New Year.

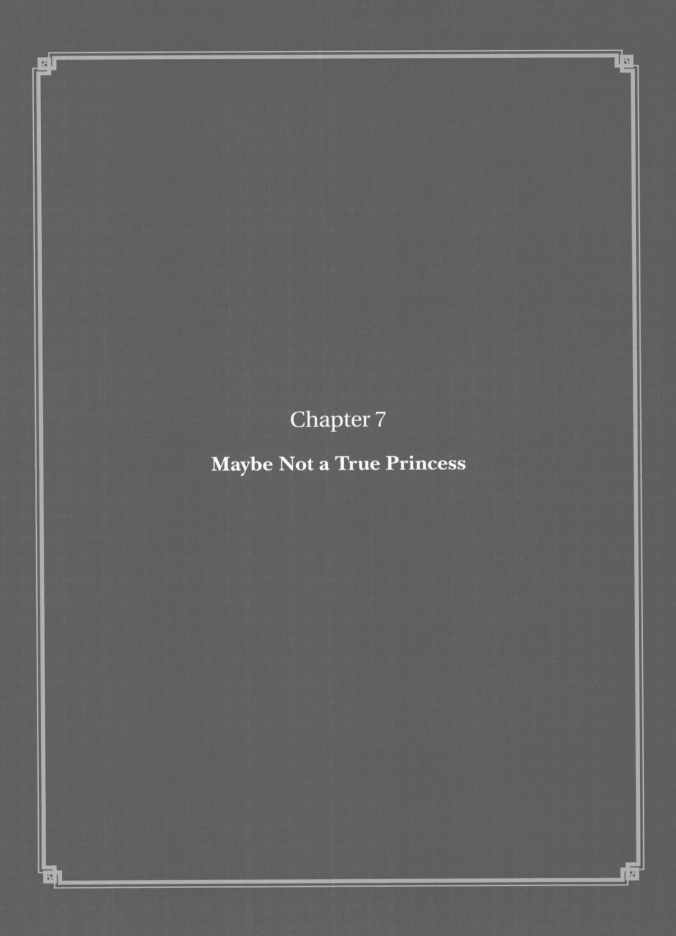

Chapter 7

Maybe Not a True Princess

When New Year's Eve came to the King's Palace, Queen Victoria was very busy with preparations for that evening. The plans for the evening were to have dinner at 8:00 p.m. and then have dancing from 10:00 p.m. until just before midnight. She had hired an orchestra to come and play live dance music. At midnight they would all gather for a champagne toast to ring in the New Year. Everyone would be dressed in fancy evening wear. It would be so elegant!

Kevin picked a black tuxedo with a white shirt, a black bow tie, and a silver cummerbund to wear for the evening. He was thinking about what he would say to Dorothy. He had just finished the book he had gotten for Christmas about the pirates and the Navy captain who'd fought against them. It was an exciting story, and Kevin imagined himself as the Navy captain, wondering how he would act if he were in that position.

That's the beauty of stories, he thought to himself. They could transport you to faraway places and take you on exciting adventures without you ever having to leave your house. Your imagination did all of the traveling for you. And yet, if the story was well written, it could inspire you to do things in real life. Of course, you had to know enough to leave the fantasy and make-believe parts in the story. But the way heroes responded to challenges in stories could help inspire you when you were faced with challenges in real life.

Kevin suddenly remembered the lovely conversation he'd had with Taryn on Christmas Eve and how they had both shared their love for stories. But he told himself that he must forget Taryn and that he would never see her again. No, he must focus on Dorothy. She was very pretty, and she was a better match for him. At least, that was what he kept telling himself.

Kevin finished dressing and went downstairs. Guests had already started to arrive. He went over to where his parents were to greet people as they came in. Soon Mr. and Mrs. Cane arrived with Dorothy. Dorothy was wearing a beautiful purple gown. It had glitter on it that made her eyes sparkle along with the gown. She was a vision of beauty. Kevin's eyes opened wide at the sight of her.

Queen Victoria said, "Why, Dorothy, how lovely you look this evening. Kevin, please show her in and help her get some appetizers before dinner."

"That will be my pleasure. Please, come with me," replied Kevin as he took Dorothy's arm.

Dorothy blushed. She was thinking that she could very easily get used to having this handsome young man at her side.

They went into the parlor where a table of appetizers had been set. There were cheese, crackers, sliced fruit, and shrimp. Kevin and Dorothy each prepared a little plate and went to sit down.

"How have you been since the other day?" asked Kevin.

"Oh, I've been very well. My mother and I went to see the Christmas ballet show. The show was wonderful. The dancing was very graceful, and oh, what beautiful costumes the ballerinas were wearing."

"Oh, how nice."

"Yes, and then yesterday we went into town to go shopping for these dresses. We went to all the best stores and tried on many different dresses before deciding on which ones to get. And then, of course, we needed to buy matching shoes."

"Oh, yes, *of course* you did," responded Kevin with a sly smile. "You know, I just finished an exciting book about a navy captain—" He started to tell her about the story, but she continued to talk about her trip into town.

"Oh, and then we went to the teahouse for afternoon tea. They had the best assortment of cookies and little pastries. We just had a great day. Anyway, I think I interrupted you. Did you just start to say something?"

"Oh, I was saying that I just finished a book about a navy captain who ran into pirates."

"Pirates! Ooooh, it sounds rather scary."

"Well, there were some parts of the story that had me on the edge of my seat. But overall, it really was a great adventure story. And the good guys win!"

"Oh, that's good." She laughed and then continued, "Oh, look at how great these napkins and plates match the decor of the room. Your mother has such exquisite taste," said Dorothy.

Just then, the butler called everyone to dinner. Kevin was happy to be going to dinner. Dorothy clearly wasn't interested in pirate stories. He would have to find some other type of stories to discuss with her.

Kevin sat next to Dorothy at dinner. But just as on Christmas, Dorothy and Queen Victoria had a lovely conversation, while Kevin and Dorothy didn't say much to each other. The interesting thing about this was that, while Kevin was keenly aware of the lack of conversation between the two of them, Dorothy hardly seemed to notice.

After dinner, King Matthew called everyone into the ballroom. The orchestra began playing a slow dance. Kevin asked Dorothy to dance. They danced together for a while, and then they decided to take a break. Kevin got a glass of punch for each of them, and they sat down.

They sat silently for a minute, and then Kevin decided to try to discuss another one of his favorite stories. "I recently read a story about the future, where people can talk to each other over long distances by holding these small devices in their hands."

"Oh, really? Where do these authors get such crazy ideas? I can't ever imagine that happening in real life. The next thing you'll be telling me is that these devices will allow people to see each other from far away too!" Dorothy replied teasingly. "Say, this orchestra is very good. I just love dancing. Let's finish our punch and get back on the dance floor."

Kevin was stunned. Dorothy had no interest at all in the things he was interested in. He finished his punch, and the two of them returned to the dance floor. But Kevin was starting to feel sad. His mind again began drifting to Taryn. He was thinking about how easy it was to talk to her and about how her eyes lit up when they were sharing their favorite stories with each other. He suddenly realized that he was making a mistake; he and Dorothy were just not meant for each other. When the song had ended, Kevin escorted Dorothy off of the floor.

"Listen," he said. "We need to talk. Dorothy, I think you're a very nice girl, and you're very beautiful. But I just don't think we have that much in common with each other. I'm sorry."

Dorothy was surprised at first, but then she said, "I think I'm the one who should be sorry. I have a confession to make. On Christmas night, I didn't really have a bad night's sleep. My father overheard your mother talking about putting a pea under the bed as a test to see if I was a princess. I knew the pea was there, so I pretended to have a bad sleep. I really slept like a baby that night!"

Kevin's eyes opened wide with amazement. *So,* he thought, *she isn't a true princess.*

But before he could say anything Dorothy continued speaking in an embarrassed tone of voice. "I didn't like lying to you. I usually tell the truth, but this seemed so important to my father. Plus, I thought that if you believed I was a true princess and married me, I would then be able to live in this nice elegant palace. I can see now that it was wrong to mislead you. And it would also be wrong to marry someone just because you like his house and parties."

Kevin didn't quite know what to feel. He said to Dorothy, "I accept your apology. I know how difficult it can be trying to please your parents, especially when they are putting pressure on you to act a certain way. I hope we can still be friends."

"Yes, of course," replied Dorothy. "Please excuse me." Dorothy left to go be with her parents.

Now Kevin felt a great relief. Since Dorothy was not a true princess, his mother would not be pushing him to marry her.

Suddenly, Kevin did not feel like being at the party. He left and went to his room. He could not help thinking about Taryn. He did go back to the party so as not to be rude to the guests, but he didn't dance with anyone for the rest of the night.

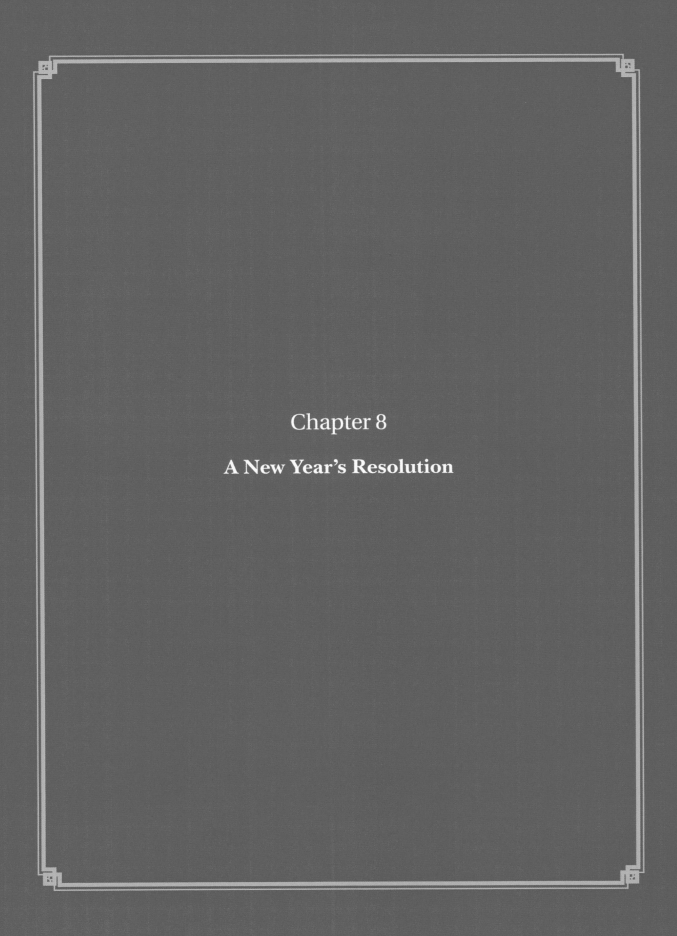

Chapter 8

A New Year's Resolution

When the New Year came at the stroke of midnight, Kevin decided that his New Year's resolution must be to find a way to see Taryn again. He wasn't sure how, but he would have to find a way. After all the guests had left, Kevin went to bed.

The next morning, Kevin was eating breakfast when Queen Victoria came into the kitchen.

"Happy New Year, Mother!" He said.

"Yes, Happy New Year to you too, my dear. Tell me, what happened between you and Dorothy last night? She spent the last half of the party standing with her parents, and you were nowhere near her. Everything seemed to be going so well between you."

"Well, Mother, the truth is that things were going well between *you* and Dorothy. She and I just did not have that much in common. We decided that it would be better if we were just friends," said Kevin.

"But she is a true princess! You shouldn't let her go just like that," protested Queen Victoria.

"Actually, Mother, she is not a true princess," Kevin explained, "at least not according to your little magical test. She knew all about the pea under the mattress, so she played along with your little game and pretended to have a bad sleep. She apologized for misleading me. She really is a nice person, but she is not for me. We would never be happy together."

"Oh, Kevin. I am so sorry," said Queen Victoria.

"Don't be sorry. I'm actually glad. You see, I think the girl I really want to be with is Taryn."

"Well, Kevin, I only want for you to be happy. I did think Taryn was a lovely girl. I was just concerned that she might not be a true princess. However, I guess my princess test didn't lead us anywhere anyway."

Kevin firmly said, "Last night, I decided that I don't care if I marry a true princess or not. I want to marry someone who cares about me and likes what I like. I think Taryn may be that girl. I just have to find a way to see her again."

Just then, the maid had come in and overheard the last bit of the conversation. "Oh, Your Highness, you just reminded me," she said. "On Christmas Day when I was putting fresh sheets on the bed that Taryn had used, I found a heart necklace on the dresser. It must belong to Taryn. I put it in my room for safekeeping, but then I forgot about it with all of the other Christmas activities."

Queen Victoria quickly said, "Kevin, you must return that necklace to Taryn. You can go today. You must follow your heart and see if she is really the girl for you."

Kevin's heart was pounding. "Yes, Mother. I will go to see her today! I'm sure she will be at home in the next village since it's New Year's Day."

Chapter 9

A Knight Finds His Princess

Kevin put the necklace in his pocket. Later that morning, he set out for Taryn's house. He rode his horse rather than take the royal carriage so as to go faster. When he got to the village, he asked for directions to the home of Taryn and James, the carpenter's family. He arrived at the house in the early afternoon.

Kevin's heart was beating fast. He was excited about seeing Taryn again, but he wasn't sure how she would react to seeing him. While he knew he felt special about Taryn, he wasn't sure how she felt about him. He was both terrified and excited as he knocked on the door.

A man answered the door and said, "Hello, young man. How may I help you?"

"Hi, I am Prince Kevin. I'm King Matthew's son. Taryn and James stayed at our house last week. I am here to return Taryn's necklace that she left at our house last week."

"Oh, yes! Please come in. Happy New Year to you, Your Highness. Taryn told us all about you. I'm her father, Joseph. We were very worried about Taryn and James. We're very grateful for the help you and your family gave her. We know how busy King Matthew must be, especially at Christmas. It was very gracious of you to take in my family. Please wait while I go get Taryn."

Taryn's father came into her room and said, "You have a visitor, my dear. A gentleman has something for you." Her father then teased her. "He says his name is Kevin or something like that."

Taryn froze for a minute. Her heart started pounding.

"Don't just stand there," said her father, "Go see him!"

Taryn began to hurry out of the room, but then she slowed down and tried to calm herself. She was thinking to herself, *Is this for real? What's he doing here?*

Taryn came into the room. Now Kevin's heart was racing fast. She was even more beautiful than he had remembered. She was dressed in a beautiful light blue dress that matched her crystal blue eyes. Her long blonde hair was flowing, and she had two braids that met in the back and were tied with a blue ribbon in such a way that they encircled her head like a crown.

"Prince Kevin, what an unexpected pleasure. Happy New Year! I'm so happy to see you. What brings you here?" said Taryn excitedly.

"Happy New Year to you too. I have your heart necklace. You left it at our house. The maid found it, but then she forgot to tell me about it until today. Otherwise, I would have brought it sooner."

"My necklace! Oh, I'm so glad you found it. I didn't know where I could have lost it. I was afraid I'd lost it in that terrible snowstorm." She walked over to him, and he handed her the necklace. "Please come in and meet my family," she said.

Taryn introduced Kevin to her parents. James greeted him as well and said he was glad to see him again. Taryn's father, Joseph, invited Kevin to stay for afternoon tea. They all had a great conversation during tea.

Afterward, Taryn and Kevin were sitting alone in the living room. Taryn said, "I finished the book you gave me the other night. It was a wonderful love story. I can see why you enjoyed it so much."

"Yes, it's one of my favorites," replied Kevin.

The two of them sat there discussing stories and the holidays. The time seemed to fly by. Soon Kevin realized it was time for him to go so that he would be home for supper. Kevin was thinking about how happy he was to be with Taryn and how easy it was to talk to her. They both liked the same things.

Taryn said, "I'm sorry to have put you through the trouble of having to come out here to return my necklace. But in a way, I'm glad it happened because I got to see you again. I must have forgotten it because I didn't sleep well that night and was rather tired in the morning."

Kevin's felt his heart leap. "You mean you didn't sleep well that night? But in the morning, you seemed fine."

"I know. I didn't want to seem ungrateful for your parents' hospitality, so I didn't say anything about it. But really, I was exhausted. I am sure it was because I was afraid that my own parents would be so worried about James and me, what with us being out in that snowstorm and them not knowing we were safe."

"Yes, I'm sure that's what it was," agreed Kevin. But inside, he was wondering if maybe it was because of the pea under the mattresses. If that were true, then that meant Taryn was a true princess after all. He had fallen in love with a true princess without even knowing it. His mother's trick had worked after all!

Kevin said, "Taryn, I have to leave now, but I was wondering if I could come back to see you."

"I would like that very much," she replied, with her eyes open brightly.

As he was leaving, he said, "May I stop by on Sunday?"

New Year's Day was a Wednesday that year, so Sunday was just a few days away.

"I will be looking forward to it," she replied as he climbed back onto his horse.

He gently brushed her cheek with his hand as he turned to head home. He glanced back to get one last look at her. She caught his eye, and then she blew him a kiss and waved goodbye. He turned his horse around and came back. Then he swooped down off the horse and took her in his arms and gave her a long kiss. She returned his embrace as he kissed her. He looked into her eyes one more time, and said, "Until Sunday!" He then climbed back onto his horse and galloped off.

She was very happy. Her prayers had been answered.

Her mother came over and gave her a hug as Kevin rode away. She said, "I told you that the Lord works in mysterious ways. I suspect we will be seeing much more of that nice young man.

"I sure hope so, Mother," said Taryn.

Chapter 10

Magic Peas?

As Kevin rode away, he was smiling all over. He galloped all the way home. When he got there, he told his parents all about his day with Taryn.

Queen Victoria was shocked to learn that Taryn had, in fact, not slept comfortably on the pea. "I guess she is a true princess after all," she said.

Upon hearing about the pea, it was King Matthew's turn to look shocked. He said to his wife, "What is this about a pea? My dear, I am surprised at you. You don't believe that old fairy tale about princesses and peas, do you? The reason Taryn couldn't sleep is because she was worried about her parents, just as she told Kevin. A true princess is tender in her heart, not in her body. And no pea can measure that. It doesn't matter how much money a person's parents have, as long as they are rich in faith and love. That is really what counts in the end. Besides," he continued, "my mother pulled that same trick with the pea the first time you and your family spent the night here for their Christmas party. It didn't work then either, as you slept like a baby all night."

"Your mother tried that on me!" exclaimed Queen Victoria. "I never knew! Oh, but you still married me anyway. Lucky for me."

"Of course, I did," said King Matthew. "I fell in love with you. Pea or no pea, you were still my beautiful princess."

"And you are my handsome prince. I guess you are right, Matthew. This business with the peas is silly. Anyway, the important thing is that Kevin is happy."

"Yes, Mother, I am very happy. Taryn likes me for who I am, not for the house I live in. And I feel the same way about her. I believe that this is going to be a wonderful New Year. I can't wait to see her again this Sunday. As Tiny Tim said, 'May God bless us, everyone,' all throughout this year and for all of our lives!"

King Matthew said, "Amen."

About the Author

Terry Boucher is a freelance writer who has degrees in mathematics and moral theology. He works in insurance during the day and teaches financial math at night. He is also very involved with his parish's adult faith formation program. Raising two daughters instilled a love of fairy tales and Broadway musicals in Terry. He lives in Connecticut with his family.